ONE LEAF, TWO LEAVES,
Count with Me!

John Micklos Jr.

ILLUSTRATED BY
Clive McFarland

 NANCY PAULSEN BOOKS

To Debbie, Amy, and John,
who inspire me to count my blessings each day
—J.M.

For my mum and dad
—C.McF.

Nancy Paulsen Books
an imprint of Penguin Random House LLC
375 Hudson Street
New York, NY 10014

Library of Congress Cataloging-in-Publication Data is available upon request.

Manufactured in China by RR Donnelley Asia Printing Solutions Ltd.
ISBN 978-0-399-54471-2
Special Markets ISBN 9780525517207 Not for Resale
3 5 7 9 10 8 6 4 2

Design by Marikka Tamura.
Text set in P22 Platten Neu.
The art was done in crayon, watercolor, and acrylic and was completed digitally.

One leaf . . .

1

2

two leaves
on the tree.

Three leaves,

3

4

four leaves,

count with me!

Five leaves,

six leaves
way up high.

5

6

Seven leaves,

eight leaves
touch the sky.

7 8

Nine leaves,

9

ten leaves,
green and young.

10

Here come
more leaves.

SPRING HAS SPRUNG!

Leaves dance gaily,
swing and sway.

Breezy, blue-sky

SUMMER DAY!

Air grows chilly,
whistling winds.

Leaves change color.

FALL BEGINS!

Ten leaves,

nine leaves
on the tree.

10

9

Eight leaves,

seven leaves,
count with me!

8   7

Six leaves, **6**

5 five leaves,
yellow, brown.

Four leaves,

4

3

three leaves,
drifting down.

Two leaves,

2

1 one leaf,
orange, red.

Soon some leaves
become a bed.

Rake leaves, take leaves,
pile them high.

Dash in.

Crash in.

Watch them fly!

Wet, wild weather
on the way.

Frosty, freezing

WINTER DAY!

Leaves lie crumpled
on the ground.

Light,
white
snowflakes

swirl around.

New buds stir
high on the tree,

growing bigger,
watch and see.

Soon green leaves from
one to ten

will sprout
and grow.

SPRING COMES AGAIN!